This Little Tiger book belongs to:

_____

_____

_____

Especially for Daniel Cautley and Max Henry with love
~ M C B

To Mum and Dad, thank you
And to my little bears, who love their porridge
~ D H

LITTLE TIGER PRESS
1 The Coda Centre,
189 Munster Road, London SW6 6AW
www.littletigerpress.com

First published in Great Britain 2004
This edition published 2005

Text copyright © M Christina Butler 2004
Illustrations copyright © Daniel Howarth 2004
M Christina Butler and Daniel Howarth have asserted their rights
to be identified as the author and illustrator of this work
under the Copyright, Designs and Patents Act, 1988
All rights reserved • ISBN 978-1-85430-976-1

A CIP catalogue record for this book is available
from the British Library

Printed in China

2 4 6 8 10 9 7 5 3

Who's Been Eating My Porridge?

M Christina Butler

Daniel Howarth

LITTLE TIGER PRESS
London

Little Bear would not eat his porridge.

"All little bears eat porridge," said Mummy Bear. "It makes them big and strong."

But Little Bear shook his head. "No porridge," he said. "No porridge."

"Then I shall give it to Old Scary Bear who lives in the wood," said Mummy Bear.

And Little Bear watched as Mummy Bear took the porridge outside and left it on an old tree stump.

That day while Mummy and Daddy Bear gathered honey from the bees, Little Bear climbed trees and watched out for Old Scary Bear.

On the way home Daddy Bear said,
"Did you see Scary Bear?"

"No," replied Little Bear with his nose
in the air, "because there is no Scary Bear!"

"Well, somebody has eaten your porridge,"
said Mummy Bear when they got back
to the bear den.

The next morning, Daddy Bear put some honey on Little Bear's porridge, but Little Bear still would not eat it. "I don't like porridge. It's horrible!" he cried.

So Daddy Bear
took it outside
and left it on the
tree stump for
Old Scary Bear.

That day, Granny and Grandpa Bear came
to stay and they all went out to pick berries.

"I hear you don't eat your porridge, Little
Bear," said Grandpa Bear. "It's no wonder
there's a Scary Bear about. Scary Bears
love porridge."

When they arrived back at the
bear den, Little Bear ran over to
the tree stump and found that his
porridge bowl was empty again!

The next morning, Granny Bear
put some honey and berries on
Little Bear's porridge, but Little
Bear held his nose and closed
his eyes. "No porridge!"
he cried. "I hate porridge!"

And so Grandpa Bear took the porridge
outside again for Old Scary Bear.

That day, Little Bear's aunt and uncle
and his two big cousins came for a visit.
    While the big bears gathered nuts
in the woods, the young bears played
Scary Bear games amongst the trees.

On the way home, Little Bear was very quiet and wouldn't speak to anyone.
"I expect he's tired," said Daddy Bear.

At supper time Little Bear wasn't feeling
hungry. Daddy Bear took him upstairs
and tucked him into bed.

That night Little Bear had a bad dream.
Old Scary Bear was chasing him through
the woods.

"I want your porridge," he growled.
"It makes me big and strong!"

Little Bear ran and ran with his porridge
… over the fields where the berries grow
… through the woods where the hazel
nuts grow and past the hives where
the bees make honey …

. . . until he came
to the old tree stump.
"You're not having
my porridge!" he
shouted to Old Scary
Bear, and he sat down
and ate up all his
porridge . . . every bit.

And then he woke up.

The next morning at breakfast time,
Little Bear ate a bowl of porridge
with honey...

. . . and then he had
a second helping
with nuts and
berries.

All day Little Bear was very busy. He helped
Granny Bear and Mummy Bear make berries
into jam and put honey into jars.

Then he went to help Grandpa Bear and Daddy Bear. But as they were storing the nuts, Daddy Bear said suddenly, "What is that noise?"

All the bears listened carefully and then they looked outside.

There in front of the bear den were lots of little animals all shouting, "Where's our porridge? Where's our porridge?"

"So *that's* who Old Scary Bear is!" cried Little Bear with a giggle.

And from that day to this, every morning
when Little Bear has eaten his bowl
of porridge, he takes another one
outside for *Old Scary Bear*.
And *he* always eats it!